THUMBELINA

by
Hans Christian Andersen

Illustrated by
Christine Willis Nigoghossian

Troll Associates

Troll Associates

Library of Congress Catalog Card Number: 78-18080
ISBN 0-89375-141-3

10 9 8 7 6 5 4

Once there was a woman who wanted a child of her own so much that she went to a witch for help. The witch gave her a magic seed, which she planted in a flower pot. Soon a pretty tulip began to grow. When the woman kissed the bud—pop!—the tulip opened its petals. There sat a beautiful child, no bigger than your thumb! "I will call her Thumbelina," said the woman.

Thumbelina slept in a walnut shell. Her mattress was made of violets, and her blanket was a rose petal. Thumbelina used a dish of water for a lake, and a tulip petal for a boat. She liked to row back and forth, singing sweetly all the while.

One night an ugly old toad saw Thumbelina sleeping in her walnut shell. "Crrro-a-k! What a nice wife for my son!" she thought. She picked up the walnut shell ... and hopped off into the garden with it!

When Thumbelina awoke on a water lily in the middle of a pond, the old toad said, "This is my son. He will soon be your husband."

Thumbelina began to cry. She didn't want a toad for a husband. Fortunately, some fish heard her crying, and nibbled through the stalk that held the water lily in place.

Away floated Thumbelina! She tied one end of her sash to a butterfly, and the other end to the lily. Soon the ugly toads were left far behind.

But suddenly, a huge beetle appeared. He snatched
Thumbelina from the water lily. He flew with her to the
top of a tree, and told her how pretty she was—even if she
wasn't a beetle. But the other beetles laughed at Thumbelina. "Where are her feelers?" they asked. "She has
only two legs—how ugly she is!" Finally, they sent
Thumbelina away.

All through the summer and fall, Thumbelina lived
in the woods. She played with the butterflies and listened
to the beautiful songs of the birds. Then autumn turned
to winter, and the snow began to fall. When a snowflake
fell on Thumbelina, it felt like a whole shovelful ... after
all, she was only the size of your thumb! She wrapped a
dead leaf around her shoulders, but she shivered as she
wandered through the woods.

One day, at the edge of the woods, Thumbelina
came upon the home of a kindly old field mouse. "You
poor thing!" cried the mouse. "Come in out of the cold!"
So Thumbelina went in and warmed herself by the fire.
Then the mouse had an idea. "If you will keep house for
me and tell me stories, you can stay here for the winter."
That was better than freezing in the snow, so Thumbelina agreed.

An old mole with a fine velvet coat lived next door.
"He will make a good husband for you," said the mouse.
But Thumbelina didn't want to marry a mole!

The mole soon came through his underground tunnel to visit the field mouse. "I have found a dead bird in my tunnel," he said. "Follow me, and I will show it to you." He made a hole in the ceiling of the dark tunnel to let some light in. There on the floor lay a swallow, still and cold.

The mole said, "Hmmph! That's one bird that won't chirp any more! I'm glad *I'm* not a bird. They just twitter about in the summer and die of cold when winter comes!" And the field mouse agreed. When they weren't looking, Thumbelina knelt down by the bird and kissed it. "This might be the same bird that sang so sweetly last summer," she thought.

That night, Thumbelina made a blanket out of hay, and crept back into the tunnel. As she tucked the blanket around the bird, she heard something. *Thump-thump! Thump-thump!* It was the bird's heart! The swallow wasn't dead after all!

Thumbelina nursed the bird all through the winter. When spring came, the swallow said, "Come with me into the forest." But Thumbelina said, "I must stay. The field mouse has been very kind to me." So the swallow said goodbye, and flew off into the bright sunshine.

Thumbelina was not happy, although it was spring.
She wasn't allowed to go outside. She had to tell stories to
the dreary old mole. And now, the mole wanted to marry
her! "You'll need lots of new clothes," said the field

mouse. Four spiders were hired to spin the thread and weave the cloth. Thumbelina was very sad. Whenever she could sneak away, she peeked out at the blue sky. How she longed for her friend, the swallow.

When autumn came, Thumbelina's new clothes were finished. The field mouse said, "Just think. Soon you'll be married to the mole." Thumbelina burst into tears. "I won't marry him!" she cried.

"Pish posh!" said the field mouse. "You are lucky to have such a fine gentleman. So don't be stubborn."

On the day of the wedding, the mole came to get Thumbelina. She would have to live with him in his dark home under the ground. But first, she wanted to say goodbye to the sun and flowers—for she would never see

them again. She took a few steps into the cornfield. The sun was shining brightly. "Goodbye, goodbye," she cried. "Tell the swallow I said goodbye." Suddenly, she heard something above her.

It was the swallow. "You don't have to marry that dreary old mole," said the swallow. "Just hop onto my back, and I'll take you far away from here!"

So Thumbelina climbed on, and the bird flew high into the sky. Far below, forests and white mountains glided by. Then there were warmer lands—with orchards, grapes, sweet-smelling air, and lovely butterflies. On and on the kind swallow flew, with Thumbelina on his back. Finally, they came to a beautiful palace in a garden near a lake.

The swallow set Thumbelina down on a large white
flower. And right in the middle of the flower was a tiny
man with a golden crown and wings! He was the king of
all the flower spirits. Thumbelina was the most beautiful

person he had ever seen. He placed his crown on her head, and asked her to be his queen. How different he was from the ugly toad and the dreary old mole! So of course Thumbelina said yes.

All at once, tiny spirits appeared from every flower, carrying presents. The best present of all was a pair of beautiful wings, with which Thumbelina could fly from flower to flower.

The king said, "The name Thumbelina is not pretty enough for such a beautiful queen. I will call you *Maia.*" The new queen smiled. And everyone was happy.

As for the swallow, when it was time to say good-bye, he flew far to the north. There, in his nest outside the window of a man who tells stories, the bird chirped the tale about Thumbelina and her adventures.

398.2   Anderson, Hans Christian 18
AND   Thumbelina.

DATE DUE	BORROWER'S NAME
3-2-95	Meganje
3-15-95	Sharon 2A
3-24-95	Angpe 1AK.
5-17-95 ²ᴬ	